OPTIC NERVE

REBECCA ROWLAND

www.maenadpress.com

FOREWORD
Write What You Want

Write what you know is the type of cliché writerly guidance you'll find splattered all over the internet. While it sounds harmless enough, go ahead and toss that slice of advice in the waste basket alongside the tab button and two spaces after a period.

Write what you WANT—now, that's where it's at.

To be good at writing fiction (without getting into the mechanics of the whole damn thing), you need to enjoy what you're writing about. If love and passion are absent when you sit before the keyboard, then your fingers will discover quite the dilemma when attempting to tap out an entertaining tale. If the author doesn't feel the exhilaration of telling a gripping tale of love or suspense or terror or heartache, then rest assured, the reader won't feel the desired emotions either.

So, yes, write what you want.

That's not say a gung-ho would-be sci-fi Shakespeare should go jotting down a hundred-thousand words on sending a rocket into space without knowing a bit about jet propulsion. Do the research if what you want to write about is out of your wheelhouse. We live in the digital age, after all. Enjoyment of what you write about is the most important thing, but not sounding like a complete buffoon is a close second.

As a quick example, demonstrating that even the greats of our field are prone to buffoonery without proper research, it still irritates the shit out of me that Stephen King, in *Doctor Sleep*, put a thumb safety on a Glock when no Glock in existence has such a thing. And shame on the editor for not finding this grievous error.

It's no big deal, right? It's just a thumb safety! Most readers wouldn't know the difference!

Wrong, I tell you. It is *just* a thumb safety, and its existence in the book bore no relevance to the story whatsoever. But what a mistake like that does to the keen reader is make them aware that the author is bullshitting them. If the author is bullshitting the reader about something as simple as a safety on a gun, it makes those more important points a little less believable. And when you're dealing in the fantastic, you *need* the reader to believe in what you're peddling.

So, again, write what you want…but do your research.

As even briefer example, would you believe Tom Clancy never served in the military? The preeminent author of military and espionage fiction never once wore a uniform. Instead, while he was selling insurance by day, he was reading up on military history and strategy then writing about it by night. He did a *lot* of research, in other words.

At this point, you're probably wondering what any of this has to do with Rebecca Rowland and her novella *Optic Nerve*. Well, I'll tell you.

Years ago, I was asked by the book's previous publisher to edit *Optic Nerve*. At that time, I did not know Rebecca and, to my knowledge, had never read any of her previous work. As I recall, I didn't know anything at all about the story going in. (Side note: I prefer going into books blind, without reading the synopsis.)

As any author who has worked with me will tell you, I'm a meticulous editor. That's not to say I'm going to butcher the author's manuscript with red ink—though, I have done this—and it's not to say I will completely rewrite the author's work—which sounds a little too cumbersome for my taste.

What I'm meticulous about, aside from your basic grammar mistakes and misused words, is getting factual information—whether it be historical, scientific, or any other factoid—*accurate*. By God, if the manuscript for *Doctor Sleep* came across my desk, I guarantee the Glock would not have had a thumb safety!

So, *Optic Nerve* came my way, and I discovered pretty quickly that I was going to be Google-searching certain things quite a bit. I would need to hit some online medical journals just to be certain about the facts. For a good editor, sometimes it's like that. I once edited a book with hundreds of references to religious texts. Another time, I worked on a manuscript in which an American author wrote a very detailed story taking place in the UK. In both cases, I looked up a lot of stuff along the way.

In the case of *Optic Nerve*, what I discovered very early on was that, while I was looking up all this ophthalmology terminology and various scientific jargon, I wasn't having to change any of it. By the time I was halfway through the book, I simply figured Rebecca Rowland, whoever she was, worked in the field. She was some genus of eyeball scientist.

You might say, she wrote what she knew. Or so I suspected.

Rebecca also—and this was even more clear—wrote what she wanted. Because *Optic Nerve*—this little novella in your hands—is damn good. It was written with love and passion and—I think—a little heartache. By the end, I was completely immersed in the story, which is something that rarely happens to editors since we're always scrutinizing those nagging details. Even now, having just read it again, I must say I'm impressed with how good it is. It's like an episode of *The Twilight Zone* that actually takes the time to get you emotionally attached to the characters, to make you love them.

Time enough at last, you might say. (Get it?)

Some months after editing *Optic Nerve*, I got to know Rebecca on social media. Not long after that, we met up at a convention, followed up by more such events. And since there's always a bar not too far from a gaggle of writers, we bought each other drinks. At some point (I don't remember when, and that can likely be blamed on Irish whiskey), I discovered Rebecca Rowland is not some Ph.D. specializing in eyeball quackery research, but an English teacher. An English teacher and a wonderful writer. She had me fooled thinking she was an expert in someone else's field. Good authors can do that.

Rebecca wrote what she wanted, and she did her research.

Now, dear reader, I turn you over to Rebecca's capable hands. Rest assured, you can believe every word, no matter how fantastic.

Patrick C. Harrison III
Author of *100% Match*
October 2024

To those who, despite Auden's warning,

try to conquer Time but instead find It deceiving them:

a love [ghost] story

But Time, to make me grieve,
  Part steals, lets part abide;
And shakes this fragile frame at eve
  With throbbings of noontide.

– Thomas Hardy, 1898

"IT'S NOT A GHOST STORY; it's a love story."

"Every love story is a ghost story. Some writer said that once, didn't he?" She leaned her head to the side dramatically and stared up at him through cat-eyed glasses, tickling the shiny wood of the bar top with the edges of her chin-length hair.

"David Foster Wallace." Shawn looked down at his drink. They were sitting in one of those fancy watering holes, the kind that served bourbon not over a shovel-full of ice chips but with one, perfectly formed block of ice, an actual geometric cube that monopolized most of the glass.

The woman seemed disappointed in his lack of attention and reached over to place her hand softly on his forearm. "So, tell me the story: love, ghost, or otherwise."

Shawn used the excuse of bringing the glass to his lips to pull his body away from her touch. He wasn't in the mood to play the game with this stranger, especially one so much obviously younger than he. In his twenties, women flirted with him because of his classic handsomeness; in his thirties, women did so because of his modest success. It wasn't until he was in his forties that he started to suspect that women fancied him because he functioned as a means to an end, a way of achieving some faraway goal: a subtle promotion, a networking connection, a temporary escape from domesticity and commitment. Now that he was well into his fifties, he no longer suspected but accepted that new partners, sexual or otherwise, always came with the price tags still attached.

He rested his glass on the cardboard coaster. "How long have you worn glasses?" he asked.

The woman frowned and appeared to think for a moment. "Hmm…I'd say since I was about ten, maybe eleven years old." She removed the frames from her face and held them in front of her. "Likely needed them before then, but I was afraid I'd have to wear contact lenses." She grimaced. "Never could wrap my head around the idea of wearing something over my eyeballs all day. The very idea makes me squeamish." She replaced the glasses and blinked rapidly. "I don't know anyone who wears these antiquated things anymore. I think it makes me retro." She smiled and Shawn looked quickly at her teeth. They were straight but unnaturally white, a tell-tale sign of home bleaching strips.

"Punctuated equilibrium," Shawn said, "is a change, an evolution in a species that comes in waves. A rapid overhaul of a trait in humans. Darwin theorized that's what happened to the appendix, that we needed it at one point, and then, it became obsolete." He swirled the ice in his glass. The edges of the cube had softened. "Later on, we found that it still has a function; it's just different from what we realized. Its usage evolved."

The woman's smile relaxed almost imperceptibly, and Shawn could see she was struggling to understand where he was going. "You're going to tell me a love story about Darwinism?" she asked.

Shawn smiled. "In a way, yes." He motioned to the bartender to bring them another round. Then he swallowed the remaining bourbon in his original glass and cleared his throat.

"JESUS CHRIST, Shawn, we've been planning this for over a month now." Maryann's voice was shrill even when squeezed through the tiny speaker, and Shawn pulled the phone away from his ear to soften it. "I think we should stick to tapas," she continued. "Everyone likes tapas."

Shawn nodded to a colleague absentmindedly peering through the window on the door to the lab. The woman glanced at the cell phone balanced on his shoulder and frowned before moving along, and Shawn returned the phone to his head. "Do you know how much more work those are?" he asked. "Let's just do a traditional cookout: burgers, hot dogs, sal—"

"I thought you weren't eating meat anymore," she snapped. "Tapas, you could make…" Shawn heard her shuffling through some papers. "…crudités, miniature macaroni and cheese and pigs in blankets for the kids, zucchini balls—oooh, and these look good: how about spinach feta wontons?"

Shawn moved the phone to his other ear. "Why don't

we talk about it at home?" He waved his hand furiously at another colleague who had replaced the woman at the window, beckoning him forward. David opened the door cautiously and stepped gingerly inside, doing his best to remain soundless.

Maryann sighed dramatically. "It's just that it's Tommy's birthday, and my mom is driving up and—" She was stretching each of the words just a hair, enough to hang a twang of her usually smothered Tennessee accent onto the plea, something she did anytime she wanted to seem folksy at dinner parties with new couples or was making demands of Shawn that were cloaked in polite requests. It was a habit Shawn had found endearing when they first met, even into their first year of marriage, but after thirteen years, he was growing to despise.

"Tell you what," Shawn said, motioning to David, who was glancing uncomfortably around the room, to take a seat. "Since you have all the recipes, why don't *you* make the crudités and the zucchini balls and the spinach…the spinach…"

"Spinach feta wontons," Maryann finished flatly.

"Right. And that's what we'll serve Saturday. I'm sure a yard full of children will find them delightful. If not, burgers and macaroni salad it is," Shawn said. He knew this was a battle that would continue after dinner that night, but one he was determined to win. His wife had been a lot of things when they first met, but a cook had never been one of them. There was nothing wrong with that, per se (certainly, most of his friends who'd remained in Manhattan after he and Maryann shimmied away to the Connecticut suburbs ordered rather than assembled their own meals) but she'd also never been much of a mother to their two boys, either, and in the last five years, she'd proved to be not much of a life partner as well.

"You'll be home by six?" she asked, the Southern accent noticeably vanished.

Shawn exhaled loudly. "Yes. To start supper. See you then." He hung up the phone without waiting to hear her goodbye.

David rubbed his stomach. "I don't know, buddy. Zucchini balls sound kind of tasty. You sure they're off the menu?"

"Keep it up and I'll tell her you have no plans for the weekend. I know how much fun a nine-year-old's birthday party can be for Gen Z hipsters like yourself."

David snorted. "So, what's up? I've been tied up in meetings all morning, but I came down here as soon as I could. Tell me."

Shawn slid into the chair opposite David's. "The CH-55? It's ready for trials."

David stood up. "Wait, what? That's six months ahead

of schedule."

"I know, I know. I just—I think I've stabilized the compound. Do you still have that friend on the Ethics Committee?"

David thought for a moment. "Yes…" he said slowly. "You think we need to fast-track it for approval?"

Shawn reached out and rested his hand on his co-worker's upper arm. "Dave, I think this could really be it. A way for people to see, just by keying into the consciousness of the people around them."

"Like bats, I've heard the pitch," David laughed. "I don't need convincing. You think Ethics will?"

"I think we're one of about a hundred firms working on this, and I want dibs on my own index entry in the science history books. Don't you?" Shawn stood up. "I mean, never mind congenital disability or presbyopia. We have a chance to get ahead of eyesight extinction, adapt our bodies before Mother Nature gets around to doing it."

David frowned. "You really believe the human race as a whole is going progressively blind."

"You don't?" Shawn tapped the mouse on his laptop and pulled up the catalog of studies from anthropology and sociology he'd compiled. "I mean, take a look at the trends.

First, there is the surge in the use of technology in the early 2000s. Then." He clicked the mouse again, and another folder opened with more downloaded studies. "A series of viral pandemics washes over the Earth in the 20s, wiping out half of the population but leaving the other half with marked reductions in visual acuity."

David leaned on the lab table. "Right. Likely due to the social distancing restrictions mandating nearly constant exposure to computer and smartphone screens for human interaction. Overuse leads to rapid breakdown."

Shawn pointed a finger in the air. "That's one theory. Another is that it is a remnant of the virus, a side effect of the body eliminating the cardiovascular aspects of the disease. Or, yet another possibility…"

David smiled. "Yes, yes, I know your belief."

Shawn raised an eyebrow at him. "Stop grinning like you just found your grandmother wearing her bra over her blouse," he said. "The Darwin theory is growing. The appendix—"

"The appendix was used to digest hunter-gatherer meals: bark, tree moss, animal hooves, things absent from modern diets, so it went somnolent, on permanent standby," David said.

"So thought Darwin. But we know today, removal of

the appendix dramatically increases the risk of developing degenerative nervous system disease, like Parkinson's," Shawn noted. "Which made me wonder: is it not that the appendix stopped being of use but rather, that it simply changed what it was being used *for?*"

David folded his arm at the elbow and rested his hand on his shoulder, a habit he often employed when he was thinking deeply about something. "You think the appendix is linked to the basal ganglia of the brain?"

"Maybe neurotransmitter production, too," Shawn said. "I don't know. No one does. Not yet. But you can bet your ass someone is working that angle, trying to solve it." He turned to his screen and brought up a document. "I think," he said slowly. "I think the appendix is just one extension of the digestive system; the other parts have since taken over that responsibility, and Mr. Appendix, here, he's been promoted, or maybe transferred to another department. He wasn't fired, just repurposed." He pointed to the screen. "The eyes are just one extension of the sensory system; specifically, one branch of the sensory subsystem of vision."

David squinted at the screen, then placed his hand on the mouse and used it to scroll down the document. "And it's being systematically repurposed. Punctuated equilibrium."

Shawn folded his arms in front of his chest. "Exactly. But if we find a way to speed up that evolution, make us adapt to this pervasive vision loss by accessing another pathway to sensing the world around us…"

"We'd put ophthalmology out of business," finished David, turning to look back at Shawn.

"That's what CH-55 does…hopefully. It bypasses the optic nerve, pushes the brain to access another sensory center, the parietal lobe," explained Shawn.

"Parietal? I thought you used the bat radar analogy in your presentation."

"Touch, taste, temperature." Shawn tapped his finger on his palm as he explained. "The three major responsibilities of the parietal lobe, right? Bats can see—the whole 'blind as a bat' idiom is misleading. But they use echolocation, the reflection of sound waves off of an object in the distance, to help *guide* their sight, especially in situations of low light, and they are nocturnal, after all."

David stood up straight again. "CH-55 helps the brain refocus its perception filter to rely on the sense of touch instead of sight."

"If my formula is right, it doesn't just help it, it will actually retrain the brain to do so," Shawn said. He rubbed his left temple.

The two were quiet for a beat. Then, David said, "Shawn, it's inconceivable, and yet, you could be changing humankind as we know it. As we see it." He laughed.

"I'm not changing it; I'm simply helping it along the path it was already going to take. If this works, it's the end of macular degeneration, of retinopathy, of Braille, of eyeglasses," said Shawn.

"It's the end of eyesight," agreed David. "And the birth of something even greater." He clapped his hands together, the slap echoing in the cavernous lab space. "I'm going to call my friend in Ethics right now. We are getting this drug on the fast track to trials. Call Linda in Manufacturing, put in an order. I know we'll have to wait on the final okay from the committee to start production for the interventional studies, but let's get a toehold in there so we're first in line when the word is in."

Shawn flashed him a thumbs-up. "On it," he said.

David walked toward the door. "I'll touch base tomorrow morning," he said, glancing over his shoulder. "In the meantime, go home and get the Tupperware ready. We both know Maryann gets her way most of the time. I'm putting in my order of leftover zucchini balls now," he smiled.

Shawn smiled back and nodded. As his colleague closed the door behind him, Shawn squatted to access the locked cabinet beneath his computer. Turning the key in the lock, he opened the door to reveal a large plastic bag of white capsules. He shoved the stash of pills into his laptop bag and began backing up his systems in preparation for going home.

"BUT I DON'T WANT to go swimming." Jessie's face was red. He had been crying all morning, something Maryann said was normal for kids at that age, but Shawn was dubious. He rarely cried as a child, never mind for hours at a time. His youngest child was so sensitive, perhaps too much so, and he was starting to wonder if it was due to his and Maryann's poor parenting.

Shawn continued to drag the skimmer over the surface of the pool. The ash tree they'd planted when they bought the house a decade earlier was already shading the edge of the water. As it shed its leaves, the stinging insects that had made the foliage their home followed. Shawn brought the net closer for inspection. In it, two tiny wasps balanced on a wet leaf, clinging to one another.

"If you don't want to swim, don't swim," Shawn said. "But I do need you to change out of those pajamas and into something presentable. Company will be here in a few hours. Sound okay?" He carefully dumped the tiny creatures onto the lip on the pool and leaned in for a better look. One of the wasps was dead, the other having clung to it in a shared attempt at salvation, or more nefariously, in a desperate panic for survival. A drowning man choking the life out of his lifeguard.

Jessie sniffed. "Can I have a hot dog?" The boy shifted back and forth on his bare feet.

Shawn frowned and glanced at the outdoor clock hanging on the wall near the patio. "Buddy, it's nine in the morning." He sighed. "How about you get dressed and come help me set up the corn hole, see if we can't get some practice in before guests arrive?"

This seemed to satiate the child. He turned and padded happily back into the house without another word. Shawn used the edge of the wet leaf to scoop up the wasps and dump them into the rose garden before heading into the house himself. Maryann was in the kitchen, scraping the mush of wet cereal from a small bowl into the garbage. When she straightened up, Shawn eyed her bare arms. They were pale, a dotting of small brown freckles sprinkled evenly along their length and tiny pinpricks of melanin filling in the spaces between them like a sepia Monet painting.

"Jessie wouldn't eat his cereal again," she said, as if her

activity warranted an explanation. "I hope Kenny and the kids can make it. You know how Jess gets when he doesn't have someone to play with."

Shawn walked to the sink and washed his hands. He hated the smell of chlorine. "If not, I'll play with him, Mae. Don't worry."

"I wish more of his friends from school could come," she said, scrunching her face into a slight pout.

Shawn dried his hands on a towel. "Who? Jessie's?"

"No, Tommy's."

"We're in the middle of June," Shawn said. "Vacations are starting. Besides, I think twelve nine-year olds swimming is enough. There's going to be enough urine in that pool by the end of the day to make it an honorary fetish ball." He pressed his fingers to his temples.

Maryann frowned. "You still have a headache?"

Shawn let his arm fall back down to his side. "It's nothing. I'm going to grab some ibuprofen. In an hour, it will be completely gone, don't worry." He closed his eyes tight. Sparks of light flashed and sizzled behind his lids, ghosts of the bright morning sun reflecting off the pool water.

Maryann's voice floated across the room in front of him. "I'll start filling up the coolers." When he opened his eyes again, she was standing by the door and kicking her feet into yellow thong sandals.

"Sounds good," Shawn said. He walked down the hall to the couple's bedroom, the soles of his plastic flip-flops suddenly muffled on the plush carpet. Once in their bathroom, he pulled open the top drawer of the vanity. The bag of white pills was buried beneath a pile of silk hair ties that Maryann had abandoned years earlier but refused to discard.

He shook one of the capsules into his palm, then retrieved the bottle of pain reliever from the medicine cabinet and dumped three of those alongside the capsule. There was a sleeve of saltine crackers on the nightstand; he'd left it there the night before when the headache had crept into his stomach and gave him the dry heaves. He grabbed two crackers from the open package and chewed them quickly. He'd never been someone who could swallow pills with water, or any liquid, for that matter; he always had to hide them in a bolus of solid food, trick his throat into accepting them under the guise of sustenance.

Once all of the medication was in his stomach, Shawn rewrapped the crackers and replaced them on the nightstand, then returned to the bathroom and locked the door. He ran his hands under the cold water, splashed his face, then stared at his bleary-eyed reflection in the mirror. He'd been taking the CH-55 surreptitiously for five days. Five days, ten pills, and only a chronic migraine to show for it. He'd considered doubling the dose but the pain in his temple was already excruciating, though so far, it had been the one and only side effect.

He cupped his palm under the running water again and brought a handful to his mouth. From behind him drifted the voice of his brother-in-law, Tim, guffawing loudly and slurring his words the way he often did after staying at one of their barbecues too long. *It's nine in the morning, for Christ's sake, Shawn thought. Here for a fucking kids' party and he's already hammered?* He shut off the faucet and dried his hands on the nearby bath towel, then glanced out of the small, sliding window above the toilet. Jessie, now dressed in a tan t-shirt and shorts, was running in circles around the back yard. No one else was in sight.

His brother-in-law's voice echoed from somewhere nearby. *I mean,* it said, *I leapt from the wagon and ran screaming in the opposite direction!* Shawn peeked into each room as he walked back through the house, but the place was empty. Finally, he exited the kitchen. On the patio, Maryann was dumping a large bag of ice into an inflatable cooler.

"Hey," she said. "Did you find the Advil?"

"Yeah, thanks," said Shawn, distracted. "Where's your brother?" He looked out at the yard. Jessie was now standing by the cement birdbath, karate-chopping the dirty water.

Maryann frowned at him. "Tim? What do you mean?" She glanced at her wristwatch. "He's not going to be here for another two hours. Closer to three, likely. He's bringing my mom."

"I thought…I thought your mom was driving straight up," Shawn said, still eyeing the backyard for visitors. "Now Tim is bringing her? You think that's wise?"

Maryann sighed and raised an eyebrow. "Trina can always drive on the way home. No big deal."

Shawn said nothing for a moment. Then, "I swore I heard him. When I was in the bathroom."

Maryann had resumed packing the ice cubes around cans of soda and bottles of water. "Who? Tim?"

"Yes," Shawn said. "Yes, Tim." He waited for his wife to respond, but she continued to arrange the drinks.

"Hey, Jess," he called out to his son. The boy stopped playing in the water and looked up. "Come help me with the games." As his youngest child ran toward him, Shawn dug his sunglasses out of his back pocket and wrestled them onto his face. It was going to be a hot day. Hot and bright.

BY THE TIME afternoon officially arrived, Shawn's backyard was filled with people: adults with their elementary-aged offspring in tow, claiming spaces of lawn with their unfolded camp chairs plopped in the shade of trees or warmth of sunshine. Children screamed and cackled, each rise in pitch a new stab into his throbbing skull as Shawn gingerly flipped each hamburger patty over and back onto the hot grate of the grill. "Mae, will you grab the hotdogs for me?" he asked without turning to look at her.

"Kids, the food is ready!" he heard her voice call out behind him.

Spinning quickly, Shawn called out, "No, no it's not. False alarm, Mae."

"What's that?" Maryann appeared on the other side of him. "Did you need something?"

"I said, the food's not done yet," Shawn said.

Maryann frowned. "Ok?"

"And…" Shawn blinked a few times. His head felt cloudy. Foggy. "And would you grab the hotdogs from the fridge? I can squeeze a few of them in right here." He pointed to the only empty spot on the grill.

Maryann rested her drink on the small table next to Shawn and walked into the house. As she did so, Jessie ran past, followed closely on the heels by his cousin Kenny. Both of them were panting loudly.

"Careful, there, kids." Shawn's brother-in-law had a booming voice, one that carried even when he didn't mean it to. When he drank, the volume grew even louder.

"Oh, Timmy, they're fine," said Maryann's mother. She adjusted the cannula in her nose and shifted slightly in her folding chair. "Let the kids play, for goodness sakes."

"Trina, grab me another beer out of the cooler, would you?" Tim stretched and rested his hand on his mother's chair. "Mom, you need anything?"

The white-haired woman smiled and patted her own knee. "Timmy, I'm just fine. Why don't you help Shawn at the grill?"

"I'm fine, Mom," Shawn said quickly before his brother-in-law could react. "Almost done here. Really." He glanced sideways at the adults. "Someone have a plate ready for Mom? I'm just about ready to get these on the bread."

Maryann reappeared with the wieners and handed them to her husband. "So, Trina, what I was saying was that Tim here was a bit of a monster in college. We both commuted, you know, because the campus was so close and Daddy being a trustee and all…"

"I commuted for the first two years, but after that, I lived off campus with the team," Tim said. "Totally fucked my grade average, too, and I mean fu—"

"Tim, please," Maryann spoke in a hushed tone. "The kids."

Tim put a hand over his mouth dramatically. "Oops. My bad. Anyhow, I was an athlete, you know, so I never wanted to screw up my game with hangovers or a beer gut or whathaveyou. Never even a drop of alcohol during the season. Off season, sure, yeah, it was crazy, but once we were in training…"

"Mae, would you grab me another plate?" Shawn interrupted. "I'm running out of room here." The sharp, stabbing pain in his head was almost blinding. If he could just get all of the food off of the hot grill and drink a glass of cold water, he'd feel better. He just needed to concentrate on moving the food…

"Tim, I don't think this is the best time…" Maryann began.

"To talk about the accident?" Tim asked jovially. "I mean,

come on, Mae, it wasn't that serious. I'm just glad it didn't fu—I mean, screw up my ride. Once Dad donated that money for the wing and—"

Trina placed her hand on her husband's shoulder. "Tim, why don't you make your mom a plate?"

"Tri, you don't understand," he stood up, swaying a little as he did. "When I say I fell off the wagon, I don't mean in the sense of a hapless sharecropper nodding off and rolling accidentally out the back," Tim continued, slapping scoops of potato and macaroni salads onto a paper plate. *I mean, I leapt from the wagon and ran screaming in the opposite direction!*" He laughed heartily and Shawn concentrated on filling each hamburger bun with a charred patty. The plate of burgers was nearly overflowing.

"Tim, seriously," Maryann said. "You're upsetting Mom." She turned to face the pool. "Kids, the food is ready!" she called. As if on cue, the boys poured up and out of the swimming pool and raced toward the patio, their towels flying behind them like capes.

Shawn, however, took two steps away from the grill and after placing the second plate of hamburgers on the short table next to him, promptly collapsed in a heap on the sunbaked grass.

SHAWN LAY IN BED, one arm folded behind his head. Maryann sat on the opposite end, rubbing greasy lotion into her feet. "How's your head now?" she asked without turning around.

Shawn looked at the ceiling. A lone cobweb waved lazily from the space just above him. He wondered if the spider that had spun it was lurking nearby. "It's better, actually," he said. He wasn't lying. After collapsing in the heat, he'd abandoned his duties at the grill for a short nap in the air conditioning, and the abbreviated rest had been just the remedy he needed. None of the parents seemed concerned or even fazed. For his Millennial generation, it was as if hosts dropping off at children's parties was par for the course. He took the second dose of CH-55 as scheduled, but the pain remained abated, at least enough to warrant forgoing another mouthful of pain killer.

Maryann lifted the CPAP mask from the holder on her bedside table and strapped it on her face. Shawn had been happy—relieved, even—when his wife was diagnosed with sleep apnea. Finally, the terrible snoring had been quelled, but he had to admit: the mask, even the quiet whisk of the air being pumped through it, was slightly terrifying to him. More unnerving was the lack of any telltale sign that Maryann had fallen asleep. Some nights, after an hour of silence and just as he was drifting off to dreamland himself, she'd spontaneously put forth a question or comment, even with the mask strapped to her face so that her speech was slightly garbled, and he'd jolt awake.

When he first heard the voice, he wasn't completely confused, not until he realized it wasn't Maryann who was talking.

"Do you believe in destiny?"

Shawn slowly opened his eyes. The television was still on, but the lights were turned off. He must have nodded off before the set timer kicked in. Either that, or Maryann had turned the lamps off manually, though he was doubtful of that. She rarely got out of bed once she was firmly strapped to the breathing apparatus. On the screen was a rerun of a 1980s sitcom, a laugh track peppering the end of each punch line.

"What did you say?" He turned to look at his wife, but he could see she was definitely asleep. In the electric alien glow, her face shone blue, then yellow.

"I said, do you believe in destiny?" the woman's voice repeated. "That our paths are already mapped out for us, every individual's act a stitch in the overall fabric of humanity…if you want to be poetic about it."

Shawn sat up and looked wildly about the room. The voice sounded like it was coming from right next to his ear. No, not next to his ear, but closer. Inside of his ear. Inside of his head, even. He looked at his wife's face again, willed the voice to continue. When it didn't, he kept his eyes fixed on her mouth and spoke out loud. "Mae, is that you?" The sound of his voice, so small and timid in the dim room, seemed foreign.

"No, not Mae," the woman's voice said simply. Not as loud as it had been. Gentle, like she was coaxing a small child or animal from a hiding place. Maryann's face remained unmoving. "So, do you?"

Again, Shawn looked around the room. He slowly slipped his feet out from under the covers and walked carefully to the bathroom. The television continued to flash rainbows across the bedroom, but he shut the door and turned on the light. His reflection in the wide mirror made him jump.

"Believe in destiny," the woman repeated. "Is that a strange question to ask?"

Shawn placed his hand over his ear. "Oh no," he moaned. The CH-55. He knew that those suffering from psychosis sometimes mistook their inner monologues as auditory hallucinations. Had the drug bypassed his parietal lobe completely, attacked the Broca area instead? Was the chemical altering his neurotransmitters? He closed his eyes and focused on inhaling slowly, then blew out his breath in a loud exhale. "Fuck," he whispered. He didn't know what emotion to feel more intensely: disappointment at the drug's failure or terror at the possibility he had dosed himself into a psychotic break.

"No, no: don't be alarmed," the woman continued. "I'm sorry. I know this is a lot to take in at once, but you're not going crazy." She paused. "Though I can completely understand why that might cross your mind."

"I—" Shawn cleared his throat. "I—you can hear me? Who are you? Where are you…exactly?" He opened his eyes and looked wildly around, then into the mirror. His hair was disheveled, but other than that, he looked perfectly normal. "You can hear what I'm thinking? Or just…you can hear my voice?" He sat down on the closed lid of the toilet.

Again, the voice softened. "I can hear you, when you talk, in your head. And when you talk out loud. But not all the time. Only when you are talking to yourself, I guess." She paused. "Try it. Think of something…think of something to eat. Something delicious. And not those overcooked hamburgers again. Gross." She laughed.

Shawn frowned. This settled it. He was definitely having a breakdown. *At least I'm aware of it,* he thought. *Can you be insane and sane about going insane at the same time?* he wondered.

"Like Schrödinger's cat?" The woman laughed again, a light, airy titter, like silver feathers. Shawn had to admit, it was a pleasant sound. "You're not insane," she said finally. "And you're not hearing voices. I mean, you are hearing *my* voice, but I am hearing yours as well. Just started to, a day or so ago. I thought I had completely lost it, to be honest, so I get what you're going through."

Shawn rested his elbow on his knee and his forehead in his hand. "This is crazy," he said out loud. "I am dreaming, or I am having a total freaking breakdown." *It's just the CH-55,* he reminded himself. He would stop taking them, and everything would go back to normal. *It's just the CH-55. It's—*

"Yeah, chances are, it's the drug," the voice said. "As a matter of fact, I *know* it's the drug. But..." Shawn heard her breath catch. Could an inner monologue catch its breath? She exhaled audibly. "Honestly...I am a bit lonely tonight. So, I'd prefer if you stuck around for a while." She laughed again, a lilting, light sound. "If you insist on thinking of me as a sprinkle of crazy or a growing brain tumor or whatever, I guess you can do that. But I swear to you: I'm not. I'm a real person. And this is as bizarre for me as it is for you."

"If you're a real person, who are you?" Shawn said.

"Helena. My name is Helena," the woman said. "And like I said, I started hearing you—just snippets, really—a few days ago. I thought it was a neighbor at first, but then I realized, you're a man. Not many of those in my neck of the woods."

Shawn thought for a moment. "You didn't think it was God talking?"

"Why would I think it was God?"

"Well, you know. Disembodied voice, male, appearing without warning…"

"I'm an Atheist," Helena said. "How did you know it wasn't God talking to you?

"Well, you're a woman."

"Ouch. Score one for the INCELS there." But she laughed again.

"No," Shawn said. "What I mean is, when people imagine God or some sort of higher power speaking to them, it agrees with their preconceived notion of what that entity is supposed to be. And even being agnostic, I grew up with those white-bearded images every kid is pummeled with." He thought for a moment. "I guess if God started talking to me, he'd be some old, dead white guy, or some ancient male figure from popular culture. A Santa Claus of reality."

"Clint Eastwood?"

"I'm thinking George Carlin."

"Would make for a hell of a colorful conversation, that's for certain."

They were both quiet for a moment. "So," Helena said. "Do you believe in destiny? I never did. Probably still don't. But it does make me wonder why you ended up on the end of my psychic line and not, say, well, anyone else."

Shawn smiled. "I am a man of science, so no, everything has to have a sort of order, a rational explanation. A place for everything and everything in its place. Reason."

"Maybe everything happens for a reason but we just don't know the reason," said Helena.

"You're saying there's a reason for this…connection?" Shawn said.

"Maybe." She paused. "That's me shrugging, but the way. I'm a visual person."

Shawn laughed. "I am going to go back to bed. This… lucid dream, or whatever it is, has to be one of the strangest things that has ever happened to me. I thank you…*Helena.*" He rose, walked over to the mirror, and raked his hair down with his fingers. He carefully pushed open the door and shut off the bathroom light, then slipped back under the covers. Maryann's breathing continued its slow rise and fall without interruption.

"Goodnight, Shawn." Helena's voice was soothing, soft.

Shawn closed his eyes and felt his body relax into the soft sheets. *How do you know my name?* he thought.

But Helena did not reply.

"HOW WAS THE PARTY?"

Shawn moved the phone to his other ear and bent down to peer into the bottom shelf of the refrigerator. He could have sworn he'd placed a gallon of orange juice in there two days earlier. Had they used it at the party? "Fine, fine," he said, shoving a forgotten bottle of salad dressing to the side. "Good weather, kids seemed to have fun." In his haste, Shawn shoved the bottle too hard and it toppled onto its side, oil leaking from the loosened cap. "Shit… hold on," he said, abandoning the refrigerator to grab something to clean it.

"Should I call you back?" David asked. "I know I'm catching you on a Sunday, but I wanted to—"

"No, no," Shawn said, dabbing the small puddle with a handful of paper towels. "Just… no, what's up?"

"Look, there's no easy way to put this," David said. "Linda says production is going to be stalled."

Shawn tossed the wad of dirty towels into the garbage

bin. "What? Why?

I spoke to her on Tuesday. She didn't mention any issues."

David took an audible sip of something, then swallowed. "Some bureaucratic red tape bullshit. Nothing to do with CH-55 in particular. Apparently, the whole system is going to be backed up. Drugs already in phase three will be delayed." He paused, then swallowed again. "I'm sorry, Shawn. It's going to happen. Just not as soon as you—we—wanted."

Shawn thought of the bag of capsules hidden in his bathroom. He had at least four more weeks stashed away, and if he needed to, he could cobble together another bottle in the lab, but in order to get the drug into trials, he needed the backup to unclog. "Shit, that's…not great," he said reluctantly. "But what can you do, right?"

David's voice was firm, even through the filter of the phone line. "Shawn, this drug could change the world. I'm not going to let it get trapped in limbo. Just hold tight. I still have a few strings to pull."

"I appreciate that, Dave." Shawn peered into the refrigerator again. "Want me to bring in some cake? Maryann ordered it from La Fiorentina."

"You don't have to ask me twice." David laughed, but Shawn's smile dropped as soon as they hung up.

"Shawn?" Helena's voice was sudden but gentle, and although it took him by surprise, Shawn did not feel startled. "Are you there?"

Shawn leaned against the sink and folded his arms in front of his chest. "Hello, my friendly brain tumor. Yes, I'm here."

"What's the matter?" her voice rose slightly in pitch, but it remained relatively low in volume as if she were trying to keep a neighbor from overhearing.

"The drug trial is stalled," Shawn said, scratching the stubble on his cheek. "Hamster fell off the wheel. You know how it is." He paused, then added, "Actually, I have no idea if you know. I guess that's just something people say. Anyway, nothing I can do about it right this second. Tomorrow, I will worry."

"What does that mean?" she asked. "Will you stop taking the CH— the CH…sprinkle of crazy?"

"And miss spontaneous auditory visits like this? No way." Shawn laughed. He pulled out one of the chairs at the table and sat down. "So, how is your day going?"

Helena laughed, a faraway tinkling sound like a Christmas bell. "Not much to report here. Say, if this doesn't sound too creepy, tell me what you look like. Tall, dark, handsome?"

Shawn glanced over at the window, seeing the ghost of his reflection in the pane. "You don't beat around the bush, do you?" He sighed. "I'm pretty average in height. Five-nine, maybe ten. You're right about the dark, but after I hit forty, it seemed like the gray hairs began to infiltrate like gangbusters." He ran his fingers through his hair self-consciously. "And the handsome, well, I think is a given. I mean, I'm a scientist. It comes with the territory." He laughed.

"Peter Parker was pretty hot," Helena agreed.

"Spider-man? That's who you immediately think of when I say scientist?" Shawn said. "Wait, isn't he a teenager, maybe mid-twenties in the comic?"

"And they kill him off. Green Goblin."

"Spoiler alert!"

The tinkling laughter again. "I didn't realize you were at the cliffhanger. But yes, you're right: he's a bit young for me, even in Hollywood standards. I'll be forty-five in the fall."

"What about you? What do you look like?" Shawn closed his eyes, hoping that the image would materialize behind his lids, but it did not.

"Well, I'd definitely have to wear heels if we signed up for dance classes. I'm five-five on a good day. Pretty plain. Brown hair and eyes. Black-framed glasses. I've always worn them, and my eyes have just gotten worse with age." She was quiet for a beat, then Shawn heard her inhale sharply. "There was an accident, when I was young—well, younger. I had to get sixteen stitches just above my right eye. I could give Frankenstein's monster a run for his money."

"Sounds attractive," Shawn quipped, but when Helena was silent, he realized his misstep. "Oh, God: I'm an ass. I'm sorry. I thought you were kidding."

"I wish I were," Helena said. "I'm making it sound worse than it is. It's just a bad scar. Doctor who sewed me up wasn't exactly an expert at plastic surgery. In the right lighting, with some makeup, no one even notices it. But it's my face, so of course, it's all I can see when I look in the mirror." Her voice lightened. "Isn't that always the case? We are our own worst critics."

Shawn stood up and glanced out of the window over the sink. Maryann was sitting in a chaise lounge, her ears plugged tight with sound buds. Although they were disguised behind dark sunglasses, he knew her eyes were closed, even as their two boys continued to disappear under the water while they played in the pool nearby. "What do you like to do? What is your favorite thing to do in your free time?"

"In my free time?" Helena echoed. "I love to read." She

laughed. "And not just Marvel comics. The classics: Stephen King. Joyce Carol Oates. Chuck Palahniuk."

"Palahniuk is a classic, huh?"

"He's not?"

"I'm not sure I've seen *Snuff* on my boys' summer reading lists, but maybe I need to examine them a little closer."

"You have children? How old?"

Shawn watched the kids chase each other around the pool. "Jessie is seven, and Tommy just turned nine this week." He smiled. "They're good kids. I know every parent says that. I mean, I'm sure even if they grow up to be murderers, I'll insist at their court hearings that they're good kids. But they truly are. Goofy but good."

"Goofy but good," Helena echoed.

"How about you? Any children?"

"No," she said quickly. "Never got the chance." Shawn heard her shift in her seat a bit. "I'm not sure I would have had the patience anyway."

Shawn watched Tommy jump enthusiastically onto a float, sending a huge wave of water out of the pool and onto Maryann, who screeched a shocked yelp followed by a stern scolding at the boy. "You learn it. If they are worth it to you,

you find the patience." Maryann stood up and looked as though she were trying to brush the water from her skin, then began to shimmy her feet into the yellow sandals lying askew on the patio. "You think you'll be around later? Maybe we can read some Stephen King together?"

"I think I can clear out some time in my schedule," Helena's voice called back, punctuating this statement with a small chuckle.

"I didn't even ask what you did for a living," Shawn said. "Don't tell me. Librarian. One of those academic ones, surrounded by ancient tomes, whose fingers race across the keyboard whenever anyone approaches with a question."

"It's funny you should say that: I always wanted to work in a bookstore," Helena said. "Too bad they are a dying institution. A dead one, really."

"As long as there are authors and readers, there will be bookstores," Shawn said. "I predict a career change is right around the corner."

"I don't know about that," Helena said. "I'm rather cemented in my ways here. I don't know if a professional adjustment is in the cards for me anytime soon."

"Oh?" Shawn watched Maryann approach the back door. "Afraid of change? You're like me. I've been at my job for more than twenty years, probably retire from the same lab—if I don't win the Nobel Prize for my breakthrough strides in pharmaceutical telepathy, that is—but I like that. I have a routine. I could probably drive to and from my office with my eyes blindfolded."

"Same here," said Helena. "But hopefully, I'll be getting out of here soon."

Maryann pulled open the screen door and walked briskly past her husband, through the kitchen, and toward the hallway. "Your turn to watch them, Dad," she said over her shoulder. "I'm going to work in my office." Shawn looked out the window again. His boys continued to play, unaware that their mother had departed.

"Shawn?" Helena asked timidly. "You still listening?"

He walked toward the back door, snatching his sunglasses from the top of the microwave as he did. "Yeah, you are stuck where you are and hope to get out. I understand more than you know: trust me." He sighed.

"No, you don't understand," Helena said. "I'm more than just stuck. I'm in MCI, Framingham." She paused. "Shawn, I'm in prison."

MARYANN WALKED SLOWLY across the wide span of lush green lawn, the glare of the sun reflecting off of her oversized dark glasses and causing a shimmer of light that temporarily blinded Shawn. He remembered being in science class in elementary school, the teacher explaining that the sun was much closer to the earth during the winter months, though for Shawn, its light always felt buffered in January and February, as if the clouds had wrapped their arms around the bright star and smothered its energy under thick bunting.

It was clearly summer: the sky was the deep, rich blue visible only in warm climates, and Shawn could see the half-moons of sweat darkening the crevices beneath his wife's breasts. She had always been a heavy sweater. It was genetic, and both of their sons had inherited the condition, their faces becoming soaked and the color of over-ripened fruit anytime they ran about the backyard in normal childhood play.

The boys were in the pool again, doing their best to run and glide in an organized circle in an attempt to form a whirlpool. Tommy began to gain on his younger brother and screeched for Jessie to swim faster. Maryann seemed oblivious to her children's action and crouched down to pour herself into a padded chaise lounge that purposefully faced away from the activity.

Shawn watched from the vantage point of the kitchen window, Tommy and Jessie's screams slightly muffled through the thick panes of glass and subtle hum of the house's central air. Tommy gave up the relentless pursuit of his brother and swam past him, purposefully splashing with his arms and legs to cause a wide ripple in his wake. The wave intensified as it traveled toward Jessie, and when it reached the small boy's face, it engulfed it and pulled his body down like a hand beneath the water, his arms flailing helplessly in an attempt to bolster himself back up from the undertow for air. Oblivious, Tommy continued his powerful push around the pool's perimeter. Jessie's head still did not emerge, though his fingers pointed erratically above the surface in a grotesque disco dance pantomime.

Shawn glanced at Maryann. She lay prone on the reclining chair, her feet splayed outward like a dancer. Her head tilted slightly to one side, and Shawn knew she was asleep. He ran from the house and out into the yard, everything slowing, the air around him palatably thicker in the muggy heat and making him feel as if he were running through mashed potatoes.

"Jessie!" he cried, though even outside, the sound strangled away, dissipated before traveling any further than a few feet from him. "Jess!" He could see splashing above the surface, but neither of his children were screaming.

The dull churn of the filter and the bubble and slosh of chlorinated water continued to rise in volume until they swallowed his cries completely. "Tommy! Jessie!"

The centrifugal force of the water sailing around the edges of the pool continued mercilessly, its surface foaming slightly, like a rabid dog. Two fuzzy outlines of tanned skin punctuated by brightly colored trunks drifted along the bottom, around and around in a darkly comical Möbius strip, their inertia ominously frightening. Shawn rushed to where the ladder had been and found that the piece had been removed, that there was no way to get into the pool and the sides were too high to push himself up.

In a panic, he turned toward his wife. "Mae, the boys, they're drowning!" he screamed, simultaneously shaking the top of her chair with both hands. "Where is the ladder? Mae, Mae! Get up, get up!" He tried to pull the chair over to the side of the pool to use as a step ladder, but it was immobile, his wife's heavy frame cementing it to the patio.

He shook the chair again and the swirl of the water stopped. A moment later, the bodies of his sons drifted up and floated motionless atop the surface, both of their faces pointing toward the blue sky, their eyes half closed and sclera milky and still.

Shawn stopped shaking the chair. He grasped Mae's shoulders and jostled her instead in anger. The sunglasses shifted on her face, finally coming askew and falling downward and onto the cement. Shawn pulled away in disgust. Hidden behind the shades had been Mae's eyes, but they weren't as he remembered them. Instead, a long gash split the top of her face in half, the bloodied laceration traveling from the middle of one ear and across her eyeballs to meet the other. From between the flaps of sliced skin pulsed a gray membrane, its slick surface heaving up and down in time with his wife's breath.

When he awoke, his back was soaked in cold sweat and his mouth was dry but tacky like he'd been gnawing on terrycloth. The image of Tommy and Jessie floating motionless on the surface of the water flashed through his memory, and he felt his stomach lurch in sick anxiety. Maryann lay on her back beside him, the airy swish of the CPAP machine her only sound.

"Helena?" he called softly. "Are you there?"

She did not respond. For the first time that day, Shawn felt truly alone.

SHAWN PAWED at the mouse on the pad as he searched the screen.

Find an inmate at a Massachusetts prison. Mass.gov.

He clicked on the link, then cursed under his breath as he read the instructions. *You will need to provide the inmate's full first and last name or their commitment number.* "Commitment number," he mumbled out loud, then looked up quickly to reassure himself no one else was in the lab. "Helena?" he said softly. "Can you hear me?"

There was still no response, so he abandoned the search page and typed another inquiry.

crimes MCI-Framingham

He clicked on the first entry at the top of the results list.

As a medium-security correctional facility for female offenders, the Massachusetts Correctional Institution at Framingham may house up to 600 prisoners of various classification levels. Seventy-two percent of the 202 inmates currently serving time at the facility have been convicted of non-violent offenses, most of them involving narcotics.

"Almost three-quarters," he whispered. What could he imagine Helena serving time for? Petty theft? Drug trafficking? What level of offense was too extreme, too shocking to imagine? Could she be one of the remaining quarter? Vehicular homicide? Battery? Murder for hire?

She sounds educated, quick-witted, he considered. An aggressive, competing thought immediately jumped onto the former. *She's the voice of your own lunacy, you idiot, and you have a PhD. Of course she's going to sound educated.* Shawn laughed out loud. Was it possible to have a dim-witted psychosis?

"Hey." David sailed into the lab carrying a white paper bag. "I brought you doughnuts," he said. "Well, I brought *us* doughnuts." He lay the bag gently on the space next to Shawn's laptop and pushed himself onto a nearby stool to look at what was consuming Shawn's attention. "Why are you researching prisons?"

Shawn clicked the yellow minimize button and the window disappeared into the bottom margin of the screen. "It's nothing. Something personal."

David raised an eyebrow. "You planning something illegal?" He unfolded the top of the bag and reached a hand inside. "For love or money? Or both? Please say it's both: the story is better." His hand reemerged clutching a Boston cream pie pastry, the chocolate ganache slick and slightly smudged along the top.

Shawn swiveled in his stool to face him. "There's something I think I should tell you."

David stared at him, his mouth frozen in mid-bite. "Uh-hm?" He quickly chewed and swallowed, then added, "I was kidding about the illegal. It's probably better for both of us if I don't know."

Shawn fingered a nearby pen and picked it up, shuffling it nervously between his index and middle fingers.

"Jesus, Shawn," David said, holding the doughnut aloft. "Out with it already. You're making it worse."

Shawn sighed and clapped his hands onto his knees. "I've been taking the CH-55."

David frowned. "What do you mean, *you've been taking it?*"

"I mean, I've been testing the drug on myself."

David thought for a moment, then said, "Okay…" He frowned again. "Wait—is this good news or bad news?" He took advantage of Shawn's response time to take another large bite.

"It's…" Shawn thought for a moment. "It's neither. I just wanted to let you know."

"And?" David looked at him excitedly. He took another bite and spoke with his mouth full. "Side effects? Sensory changes? Tell, tell."

"Oh, there've been sensory changes." Shawn tapped the pen against the top of the lab table. "That, or I am quickly developing a brain tumor."

David brushed his hands together. "Not funny. Tell me what's going on."

Shawn summarized the events from the previous week, leaving out the details of the nightmare, even though its images were still fresh in his mind. "Look, I know it sounds crazy, and maybe it is. Maybe *I* am. But *something* is happening with this drug, Dave. I have to ride it out, see where this goes."

David stared at him for a moment, lost in thought. "How's the headache?"

"Barely there. Most hours, completely gone."

"And the voice, this Helena, you sense it's coming from where? Inside your head? Externally?" He pushed the white bag toward Shawn, who shook his head. "What about your vitals? Have you been checking your temp, BP, heart rate? Any pupil dilation?"

"It feels internal. Almost like my own thoughts, but louder. Clearer." Shawn rubbed his hands on his thighs. "I thought it was Maryann at first, but now that we've spoken over and over, I can tell the difference. The only thing I can equate it to is when I was in college and took this twentieth-century drama course to fulfill my humanities requirement. Reading a play is not like reading a novel. It's all dialogue, so you kind of have to *hear* the characters in your head as you read it, or it doesn't come together." He smiled. "I know, I know it sounds crazy. But I am telling you, this woman is real. Somehow, the drug is triggering an area of the brain we haven't used before."

"We're all going to be mind readers now," David said. "There goes my poker night."

"But that's just it," Shawn could hear his voice grow more excited. "It's not everyone, it's this one woman. And she's three hours away." He glanced at his laptop.

David followed his eyes and made the connection. "This woman is in prison? You're hearing voices and they're from convicts."

Shawn cleared his throat. "*One* voice. *One* convict."

"Well, that's so much better. You said you heard your brother-in-law hours before he was in your home, though. And then Maryann before she actually spoke."

Shawn shook his head. "My head was screaming. I don't know what I heard. But since then, it's only been this woman, this one woman."

The two men were silent for a beat. Then, David offered, "Do you hear her now?"

"Is this my cue?" Helena's laugh tinkled softly in his ear, and she continued, more seriously, "I'm sorry. I wasn't eavesdropping. Well, not really."

"Yes," Shawn said. "I hear her now. It's not constant. I can't explain it. I have to let her in. It's like a mental arm, reaching out. I can break the connection just as easily. The first time, I didn't even realize I was doing it until we stopped our discussion and I could sense the shift."

David leaned closer. "But you're the only one taking the CH-55, right? So how is this woman able to connect? Why her? If the drug is awakening the parietal lobe in ways we haven't before, how is it that this…*Helena*…has the ability as well? Is it new for her, too?"

Shawn was quiet, listening. "Yes, according to her, she just began hearing me one day. And only me: it's not like she can do it with anyone else."

David eyed the white bag.

"Take the other doughnuts, for God's sake. You know I'm

not much of a sugar person. Stop using me as an excuse for your sweet tooth," said Shawn.

"Ah ha!" David laughed. "Now you're reading my mind, too."

"No, I've just been your friend forever."

David smiled, but he looked hard at Shawn. "You know I need you to have a full work-up. Today. Not tomorrow or any of this, later-in-the-week bullshit. fMRI, blood work, the whole kit and caboodle." He slid from the stool and grabbed the white bag. "Officially, I can't authorize you to continue this experiment. Christ, Shawn, you could stroke out, you could be causing permanent dementia for all we know."

Shawn looked straight at David, resisting the urge to lower his eyes in shame. "I'm still glad I told you."

"I am, too." He began to walk toward the door, glancing at his watch as he did. "I'm calling Sheila now. It's almost ten. I want you downstairs, in radiology, before noon. No excuses."

"None from me," said Shawn.

David rested his hand on the knob but paused before turning it. "A part of me, I admit, is damn excited about this, Shawn. But a much bigger part is pissed. I know you're a big reader. Didn't you learn anything from Jekyll and Hyde? Frankenstein? Dr. Moreau?"

"Back in the late twentieth century, an Australian doctor named Barry Marshall drank a solution containing H. Pylori in order to study gastric disease. Because of him, we have antibiotics to treat peptic ulcers. A half century before that, pharmacist Albert Hofmann combined lysergic acid with extracts from a medicinal plant used by ancient cultures, and boom! The flower children of the sixties' favorite tune-in-drop-out vehicle was born." Shawn shifted his torso back toward his laptop.

"And for every Gregor Mendel, there is a Brundlefly." David opened the door. "Before noon. I mean it."

"YOU CALL yourself a Stephen King fan, and you've never read *Night Shift*?" Shawn said, resting the open book on his chest. The pages were soft, like worn cotton, and significantly yellowed with age.

"I jumped on the horror train late, I'm afraid," Helena said. "And the selection here is… well, limited, I guess is a nice way of putting it." She laughed. "I read all of the last novels he wrote, though."

Shawn cleared his throat dramatically. "Ahem. Well, my dear, you are in for a treat. This was my favorite short story collection growing up. So many of the stories were turned into movies: *Children of the Corn, Graveyard Shift, The Lawnmower Man*…of course, that last one: I don't know what the hell King was thinking when—"

"Are we filming a documentary on the book? Make with the reading, man!"

"Okay, okay," Shawn laughed. "So pushy." He adjusted the

reading glasses on his face and began to thumb through the pages, scanning the headers for one tale in particular.

"Hey," Helena said softly. "Thanks for reading to me."

"I told you: it's my pleasure. I just wish you had made this request from the get-go. I'm already making a mental reading list and gargling salt water in preparation for this routine."

"No," she continued. "You don't understand. I love to read. Always have, really. But my eyes aren't what they used to be. Just part of the rapid degeneration the human race has suffered over the past decades, I suppose."

Shawn sat up excitedly. "That's just it: that's what I was working on when I created the formula for CH-55: a cure for blindness."

"I hate to be the voice of reality, Shawn, but I think your recipe needs a few tweaks."

Shawn laughed. "Yes, of course, but I think I'm in the ballpark. I can just feel it. You'll see: you'll be seeing again, good as new, before you turn fifty, if I have my way."

Helena's voice was soft again. "You think so, huh?" She sniffed.

"I know so. But, until then, you'll just have to suffer with your own private Audible narrator, yours truly."

"I like it, actually," she said. "Hearing your voice in my head is like reading, really: it's the same feeling of hearing that cadence of the author's words and sentences as I read silently to myself." She paused. "Yeah. I like it a lot."

"Well, sit back and enjoy the show," Shawn said, "because this one is called *The Boogeyman*."

When he was done with the story, Helena was so quiet, he had to check that she was still there.

"You read this when you were growing up?" she finally answered. "How old were you, exactly?"

Shawn thought for a moment. "I don't know. Maybe sixteen."

"That is one of the scariest stories I've ever heard," Helena said. "Seriously. It's a good thing there are no closets here. At least, not in my cell."

Shawn was quiet. "Where are you, really?" he asked softly. "I can't believe you are really in prison."

"Why?" He heard a slight edge to her voice, a defensive barrier. "People aren't all bad here, you know."

"And people can change."

"Yes," she said. "They can. And do." They were both quiet for a moment. "As a matter of fact, I read somewhere that the human body replaces itself every seven years, so the people we are at thirty or forty are light years away from the people we were as kids or even young adults. You're a different person than the boy who first read this story, four times over."

Shawn smiled. "Seven years is kind of an average, but yeah, you're basically right. Skeletal muscles cells regenerate every fifteen but red blood cells only last about four months." He turned his head to glance at himself in the mirror above Maryann's bureau. "But true all the same. I'm nowhere near the same person."

Helena paused, then: "It's a good thing. I don't want to know what kind of psychopathic kid it was who relished reading about child-killing monsters creeping around in bedrooms." The tinkling laugh followed, but it was somewhat stilted.

They were quiet again, then Shawn asked, "What is it like, being in prison? I mean, what do things look like around you?" He paused. "Is that a silly question?"

"You mean, is it like it appears in the movies?" Helena asked. "In a way. Everything is much brighter, though. I'm talking white walls, artificial lighting that highlights every speck of dust or faded stain. Blanche Dubois would drop dead from fright!" She laughed. "In the movies and shows

I've seen that feature prisons, the places always seem so dark. Here, I can't help but think, is this part of the rehabilitation, making everyone squint?"

"Kind of like the weirdly dark lighting in police stations—especially the interrogation rooms—in TV crime dramas," Shawn said. "I always think, maybe cat burglars wear dark clothing not to commit the crime but in case they are caught, they could just hunker down in a corner of the station and no one would find them!" He caught his laughter, remembering that he didn't know what had warranted Helena's incarceration, but she giggled appreciatively.

"Agreed," she said. "I want you to know, Shawn, I'm not the same person I was years ago."

Shawn was silent, listening.

Helena sighed. "I hurt someone. I didn't kill her, but I hurt her enough physically, caused enough pain and scared a lot of people enough to warrant my punishment. To this day, I don't know what came over me. I was a straight-A student, worked a part-time job, was saving up for college. I didn't have many friends, and certainly, not anyone romantic, but I studied hard and worked hard…and I had my whole life ahead of me. And then…" Her voice caught. Shawn heard her swallow hard and collect herself. "And then," she continued, "there was this couple, and something pushed me to…" Her voice trailed off. Shawn thought he heard a small sob.

"Please…" he said gently. "I'm sorry. I shouldn't have asked." She sniffed and cleared her throat but said nothing.

"I know you're not the person you were as a teenager," Shawn said. "I like who you are now, and that's all that matters."

Both were quiet for another moment. Finally, Shawn asked, "Can I visit you?"

"No." Helena's voice was sharp, resolute.

"Why not? I did my research. You need only put me on your visitors' list. You're only a few hours away, and—"

"No, Shawn," Helena said, though her voice was subdued. "We can't see each other. Look, we wouldn't be able to touch anyway. Isn't this communication, this ability we've harnessed, isn't it more intimate?"

"Intimate? I don't even know your full name," Shawn said, and as soon as he did, he felt ashamed, silently acknowledging his ulterior notice for the comment. He did not retract his statement, however, but held his breath, waiting.

"It's Wells," Helena finally said. "Helena Georgia Wells."

"Wells? Like Dawn Wells?"

"Who is that?"

"You know," Shawn said. "Mary Ann from *Gilligan's Island.*"

"You've lost me," said Helena.

Shawn laughed. "You're kidding. You never watched reruns of *Gilligan's Island* as a kid?"

"Shocking, I know," deadpanned Helena. "And to think social scientists have been studying criminal behavior for centuries when the catalyst all along was a lack of popular culture exposure." She added the tinkling laugh. "I always told people, *Wells, like the beach,* the one in Southern Maine just north of Ogunquit. I had an aunt and uncle who lived nearby, and my parents would take us there every summer." Her voice took on a dreamy quality, and Shawn leaned back on the bed as she continued. "When you're a kid, everything is possible. Your whole life is right there, waiting, and you can be anyone you choose. I liked to pretend the place was my kingdom, that it was named just for me. I must have bought every tourist shirt in that beachfront souvenir shop!"

"I can imagine," Shawn said. And for that instant, as he lay on his back, staring at the cobweb on the ceiling, he could.

"WHY DO you always call when I am looking in the refrigerator?" Shawn asked, sandwiching the phone between his ear and shoulder.

"You're the Amazing Kreskin. No wait: the opposite of the Amazing Kreskin. You can send your thoughts to others, make them know things," said David. "You're the Bizarro Kreskin."

"Maybe I'm just always hungry." Shawn grabbed a tub of store brand hummus and turned it over to check the expiration date. "To what do I owe this pleasure, in the middle of a Saturday?"

"I spoke with Sheila yesterday afternoon. I tried you in the lab but you'd left for the day."

Shawn pulled the cover from the hummus and opened a cabinet, searching for crackers. "Yeah, I had to pick up the boys and Mae's car is in the shop." When he found the box he sought, he pulled it from the shelf and attempted to open it with one hand. "Why?" He stopped fumbling with the inner packaging. "Oh, no. Should I be sitting down?"

"No, no, nothing like that," said David. "Just… some strangeness. You have to pop down there on Monday and see the scans yourself. They are pretty remarkable."

"Remarkable like how?"

"In the fMRI, the tech had you engage with visual stimuli, correct?"

"Yes…" Shawn piled the box on top of the tub of hummus and carried the two, tray-like, to the kitchen table. He pulled out a chair and sat down. "I mean, that's not all they had me do, but that was a part, sure. To test the neural pathways."

"Right. Can I ask you something?"

"Of course."

"Did your telepathic pen pal talk to you at all when you were in the machine?" David's voice sounded slightly amused, but it had an edge of severity to it as well.

Shawn thought of Helena. He wondered if she were listening in to their conversation. She claimed not to be able to eavesdrop without him knowing, but he wasn't sure that was completely true. "Yes. Not the whole time, but yes, part of the time."

"Did you talk back?"

"I didn't want to look like a lunatic, so no, I didn't."

"I don't mean out loud necessarily, but with your mind? Are you able to do that?"

While lying still in the cumbersome medical apparatus, Shawn had tried to carry on the conversation with Helena completely in his head, but he found the process exhausting. It required a strange kind of physical exertion, to reach out with his brain and communicate. Speaking out loud was like releasing the floodgates on a vat of his thoughts: everything flowed effortlessly, although he knew this was, in part, because Helena seemed to understand him so well, he didn't feel the need to hide or filter anything with her. Whatever came to his head, he could let out. "I am, and yes, I did try while I was in there, but the conversation wasn't very long. Why do you ask?"

"Let me ask you this. When you were asked to focus on visual stimuli, what part of your brain would you expect to light up? The occipital lobe, right?"

"The temporal lobe in general, but yes."

"It did…initially. But as the scan continued, the blood flow shifted and became centralized in another area."

"Let me guess," Shawn said. "The parietal lobe. That's what we were trying for, Dave. We've talked about that."

"No. Not the parietal lobe." David was silent.

"Are you being dramatic? What part? Tell me."

He heard David take a deep breath. "There was activity in frontal cortex, basal ganglia, parietal cortex, cerebellum, and hippocampus. Nothing off the charts, but unusual for an isolation activity." David cleared his throat. "I need you to be up front with me, Shawn, okay? This is off the record."

"Alright," said Shawn quietly. His stomach churned audibly, but not from hunger.

"Since starting the CH-55, have you had any problems with memory? Attention span? Motivation?"

"Motivation? What? No, no, none of that. Why?"

David cleared his throat again. "Sheila says that for a few minutes, a quarter of the screen looked like a forest fire: orange and yellow crackling in a very isolated section of the scan. The dorsolateral prefrontal right cortex."

Shawn thought for a moment. "That's the region of the brain associated with all of those things, working memory, selective attention…but that doesn't make sense. I'm not having any issues with those areas."

"What about time?" David asked.

"What—what *about* time? What are you asking?"

Shawn heard David readjust the phone. "Are you having any issues perceiving time, or perhaps experiencing time passing faster, slower? Does anything about it seem different to you?"

Shawn glanced at the clock on microwave's display. "No. Nothing." He dug his hand into the box of crackers and pulled one out, a star-shaped biscuit. He dipped its edge into the open container of hummus and pulled out a small dollop. "David. I like this feeling. To be honest, I don't really care if my neurons are misfiring." He shoved the cracker into his mouth and chewed.

"Maybe I need to check Sheila's report again. What is the part of the brain associated with rational thought?" David asked.

Shawn swallowed and lowered his voice. "Look…I don't expect you to understand. It's just that I finally—" He looked around the kitchen and listened for anyone lurking in the next room. "I am forty-one years old. You know that feeling, when you're young and you meet the girl, or the boy— the *person* of your dreams? Not necessarily your dreams, but someone who you really connect with, who seems to know you without actually knowing you?"

"Those are hormones, Shawn. You're talking puppy love and puberty."

"No." Shawn put down the round cracker he'd pulled from the box. "This is something different. I can't explain it accurately. It's as if—it's as if this woman and I knew each other a long time ago and we've been reunited, or maybe that we've known each other a long time, and I…" He fingered the edge of the cracker, pushing it slightly forward on the table. "I sound like an ass. I don't know. It's something. A connection. A feeling. I like it. I like this feeling. I don't want it to go away."

David laughed. "You sound like you're in love."

"Maybe I am," Shawn said. "Or at least, infatuated. No, more than infatuated. Maybe I *am* in love." He spoke this louder than he intended, as if he were engaged in a heated argument with himself.

David was quiet for a moment. Then, "How does *she* feel?"

Shawn broke the cracker in half and stuck the jagged edge into the dip. "I think she feels it, too."

"Then what are you waiting for?" David asked.

"She's in prison, Dave," Shawn said.

"Not forever," David said. "You said she mentioned she anticipates being paroled someday? I can only assume it's sometime soon."

Shawn tapped the table with the other half of the cracker. "Yes, true."

"Go there. To Framingham. She can't refuse to see you if

you are parked outside after you drove all that way," David said. "If she still does, you know she's, well, you know she doesn't feel the same."

Shawn ended the call and rose to return the box of crackers to the kitchen cabinet. When he did, he looked over at the back door leading to the yard. Maryann stood on the other side of the window, partially obscured by the half-closed blinds. Shawn watched as she met his eyes for a long second, then turned around and walked back towards the pool.

THE FOUR OF them sat at the dining room table. Outside, a storm raged, mercilessly beating the vinyl siding with sheets of rain. Inside, the room was dim and the windows black. The formal occasion taper candles, the ones Maryann saved for holidays like Christmas and Thanksgiving, were lit, their glow casting odd shadows on the small boys' faces.

In the center of the table, a wide silver chafing dish covered with an ornate top reflected their skewed images while blue fire from two Sterno fuel cans licked its bottom. Settings of fancy wedding china and silverware lay before each person, yet Tommy and Jessie sat comfortably in their seats wearing only t-shirts and swim trunks.

Tommy leaned over his dish, grasped the handle of the chafing cover, and pulled it dramatically off. A rush of steam puffed from the plate and Shawn leaned forward to get a better view.

Inside, sitting snug within a shallow bath of hot water, sat a human brain: not pieces, but the whole skull filling, like one of the plastic models Shawn remembered from college anatomy classes. Jessie reached out with a massive serving fork and began to poke sections of the grayish-brown organ as if testing its tenderness. After a few awkward jabs, the lobes responded, lighting up in a rainbow of colors: first red in one part, then yellow in another, followed by green and blue until it began to resemble a childhood toy of Shawn's, an electronic memory game. Blinking red-red-green. Blue-yellow-blue-red.

"Who are you talking to?" asked Maryann, but she wasn't speaking to her child or to any of her family members. She was speaking to the brain in the dish. "Shawn? Shawn?" she repeated, then snatched the cloth napkin from her lap and threw it angrily to the floor. She began to rise, but as her spine straightened, something seemed to grip her torso and wrench it in place. She paused, her shoulders still slightly hunched, and looked at Shawn wordlessly in terror.

"Mae?" Shawn called, standing up from his chair. "Mae?" He walked toward her, but the distance between his end of the table and hers elongated like a fun house mirror. His feet moved forward, but each attempted step cemented him harder in place. Jessie continued to jab at the brain and Tommy soon joined him, the two of them piercing and poking the membranous oddity until it lit up in rainbows like a disco floor.

Maryann's hands clawed at her throat and her eyes widened in silent panic. Beneath her fingers, a long dark cut traced a path from her neck to her sternum. The gash opened and dark red blood poured from it, seeping out from between the digits and dripping down her wrists. Maryann clutched harder as if trying to hold the flaps of skin together, a bizarre pantomime of a woman having been caught off guard wearing only a tiny slip of a robe, or an obese comedian trying to button close a dress shirt two sizes too small. Her desperate attempt failed miserably as the skin peeled apart and the pulsing musculature pushed forward, its surface wet and sticky, the color of an overripe plum.

Shawn grabbed his youngest son's arm by the wrist and wrestled the serving fork from his grasp, and his other son withdrew his utensil from the brain's gray flesh, holding the knife in mid-air. Shawn looked again to his wife, but she was no longer looking at him. She was no longer looking at anyone. The crevice in her chest snaked its way up her face, then branched out to each of her eyes, piercing, then slicing them in half. The brown irises flooded with blood, and Shawn began to scream.

He was still screaming when Maryann tore the CPAP mask from her face. "Shawn?" She was shaking him nervously, still planted firmly on her side of the bed but keeping a safe distance.

"Shawn?" Helena's voice peeped cautiously inside his head.

Shawn sat up and covered his face with his hands. He didn't answer either woman. He was too focused on willing the images of the dinner party to disappear forever from his mind.

FIND a massachusetts inmate

Shawn typed the query into the dialogue box and hit Enter. His previously visited site was highlighted in purple. *Find an inmate at a Massachusetts prison.* He clicked it then completed the short inquiry form with Helena's full name. Immediately, a box popped up warning him that incarceration records were not to be used in an unlawful manner or to stalk or harass others. *Well, Massachusetts, considering we're able to transport our consciousness into each other's heads, I think we're way past that question.* However, as he hovered the mouse over the red *I Agree* button, he paused.

Do you really want to know? Shawn asked himself. Of course, it was perfectly understandable for him to be curious about for what his nearly constant companion had been sentenced; Helena's details on the event had been minimal if anything. *Though once you know, you can never un-know, know what I mean?* his thoughts elbowed him in the gut like a vaudeville player.

He pushed the warning aside and clicked the red button.

No offenders matching your criteria were found.

He must have misspelled her name. He tried again.

No offenders matching your criteria were found.

He entered the name again, rearranged a few letters, added a letter, subtracted one: all possible versions and combinations that he could fathom. The response remained the same. Finally, he clicked the link *Possible reasons the offender is not listed.* The resulting page provided a laundry list of why Helena's name had not appeared: she was a federal inmate, her records were part of a county not participating in the database, the database itself was down.

Shawn shut his laptop in frustration. He glanced out of the window. Maryann's car was not in the driveway; she was spending the day at a spa appointment and promised to pick up the boys from their baseball practice on her way home. The house was silent save for the faraway ticking of the grandfather clock in their main entranceway.

"Hey," Helena's voice appeared suddenly. "I'm so sorry I'm late. I've been looking forward to talking to you all day. I'm excited for my story. You promised a Joyce Carol Oates this time. *Big Momma*, I believe? I—"

"I tried to find you in the state prisoner database." The

sentence came out so emotionless, so matter-of-fact, Shawn surprised even himself with the flat tone.

"You did what?" Helena's voice changed as well. The disappointment was palpable, but it simmered beneath something else. Fear, perhaps? Shawn wasn't certain.

"I went into the state search engine and looked you up," he said. "People check each other's digital footprints all the time, especially strangers they begin dating. And, like you said, we've developed a kind of intimacy that I thought…" he paused. "That I thought maybe warranted it."

"You searched for me in a prisoner database, though," Helena said. "Not just online."

"Yes," Shawn said. "Why? Were you featured in a heartwarming hometown news story I might stumble across?" The comment had a sharp edge to it, a meanness he only heard from himself when he argued with Maryann.

"No." For the first time since it had appeared in his head, her voice sounded far away.

"I just want to know you, Helena," Shawn said.

"You do know me. You are getting to know me," she answered.

"Are you really in prison? Tell me the truth," he said. "Please."

"Yes," Helena said quietly. "I really am."

"Then why can't I come visit?" he asked, his voice rising in volume, sounding strangely alien in the empty, silent house. "Why won't you see me?"

"It's just not that easy," she said. "Why is this so important to you?"

"I don't know," Shawn blurted out. "I feel things with you I haven't felt in a very long time. I want to know more about you. I want to know everything."

Helena let out a long exhale that bordered on a sigh. "You don't understand—"

"Make me understand," Shawn interrupted. "I'm not going to take a drug for the rest of my life so that I can talk to you. Not when you are out in the world and only a few hours away. I'm grateful to CH-55—I am—but this isn't what it was intended to do, and—"

"I know, Shawn," Helena said. "I do. Please know, I do."

Maryann's car pulled slowly up the driveway, the outlines of Jessie and Tommy in perpetual motion along the back seat. On reflex, Shawn smiled to himself, watching them. Before he knew it, they would be teenagers, their whole lives ahead of them. The older they grew, the more excited he was for them and the possibilities that lay before them.

"Shawn?" Helena called.

"I'm here, but I have to run," Shawn rubbed his face with one hand. "I'm sorry: I shouldn't have wasted our time together, cornering you." He opened up his laptop once more and typed in the password to unlock it from sleep.

"Tomorrow is the third of July, isn't it?" Helena asked quietly. "You have anything planned for Independence Day?"

Shawn heard the stomping of his son's feet as they clamored through the back door. "Nothing special. Just a cookout here at the house. Wife, kids. I have to go to the store tomorrow and pick up the food."

"Shawn, I want to let you know: I really enjoy our time together. Would you do me a favor?"

"Anything."

"Pick me up a card. You can mail it to me."

Shawn laughed. "Like, a greeting card? Does anyone under the age of seventy-five do that anymore?"

Helena laughed. "I'm an old-fashioned gal, I suppose," she said. "Address it to me here. I'll get it. I promise. But don't write anything romantic inside, okay? Sometimes they read our things. Just…keep it light."

"I'll write that you're special," Shawn said, "so that if you ever need a reminder, you'll have one. Until I can tell you in person, that is."

He heard her tinkling laugh again, but it was strained.

DON'T FORGET RELISH. Dill, not sweet.

Shawn glanced at the text message from Maryann on his screen. The all-in-one department and grocery store, one of thousands in a discount chain dominating the country, was a sea of customers dressed in shorts and weekend gear, all of them piling their shopping carts with picnic necessities and outdoor activity accoutrements in preparation for the holiday. Some talked incessantly on their phones as they scanned the shelves; others seemed to be on solemn reconnaissance missions and focused their attention pointedly on the sale racks and hand-written lists they clutched in their hands.

Shawn scanned the shelf in front of him. There were jars of pickles—all kinds of pickles: spears, chips, halves, even pickled okra and carrots—but no relish. He wondered if he would have better luck in the condiment section. He pushed the cart further down the aisle. At the other end, an older woman held a cell phone horizontally in front of her face and screamed into it, the caller's response clearly audible from thirty feet away. Shawn hated shopping on the weekend, never mind on one that abutted a big holiday, but he hated when people conversed on speaker phone in public even more. He closed his eyes and took a deep breath, the growing cacophony rising around him, choking him like tear gas. The lightweight coat he'd thrown on in anticipation of the chilliness in the overly-air conditioned warehouse seemed to tighten around his torso like a strait jacket.

"This is one thing you probably don't miss: shopping in a mobbed store," he said out loud, keeping his mouth as tight as possible in the hope of disguising the appearance of talking to himself. On second thought, he realized it might fortuitously keep other customers at a distance. He made up his mind to simply ignore any strange looks.

"I was never a fan of crowds," Helena said. "Or lots of activity. When I was a kid, maybe seven or eight, I played on a soccer team. I was never any good, really; my parents made me join. They wanted me to stop burrowing myself in my room to read books. Anyhow, I remember this one game where there were like, ten of us, all gathered in a tight formation around the ball, everyone kicking and kicking, trying to get it out, but there were so many players, there wasn't a spot of daylight where the thing could escape so the ball just kind of stayed there, trapped within a mass of banging cleats. This continued for what seemed like an hour, though in reality, it was probably just two or three minutes."

The sound of Helena's voice was an instant panacea to his panic; Shawn felt his shoulders relax and his breathing calm. "Still. Sounds intense. How did it end?"

"All of the girls were screaming," Helena continued. She paused for a moment, as if watching the moment on a screen in front of her and delineating the action, frame by frame. "All of us within inches of one another, everyone screaming so loud, I thought my eardrums would explode. Finally, I don't know why, but I just leaned down and picked up the ball with my hands and clutched it to my chest."

Shawn spotted the containers of relish and dropped a plastic squeeze bottle of it into his carriage. "Wait: you picked it up? With your hands?"

"Yes, yes," Helena said. "I know. The referee blew his whistle, and all of the girls in the mob stepped backward a few paces and stared at me in disbelief. One of the girls—she was the bully on the team, her name was Laura, I recall—yelled at me, asking if I was stupid and what was wrong with me. It wasn't until then that I let the ball go, let it bounce to the ground." She emitted a long sigh. "The opposite team got a free penalty kick, but they didn't score on it, thank goodness.

The strange thing is, I can't explain what made me do it, except I just wanted the noise, the battling, all of it to stop."

Shawn frowned. "That is a little odd, I mean, looking back now. Right?"

"I suppose." Helena was quiet for a beat. "I remember being in the car with my dad, after the game. I was mortified. We won, but my teammates shunned me, either out of disgust or discomfort. I felt awful and alone. And then, all my father said on the ride home was, *Why on earth did you do that, Helena? Why?*" Shawn heard her swallow. "Sometimes, things just happen, I suppose."

"I think you answered your own question," Shawn said. He angled the cart around a display in the main thoroughfare and headed to another section of the store.

"What question?"

"*Do you believe in destiny?* Remember? It was the first thing you said to me."

Helena laughed: an easier one this time. The tinkling sound. "I'm still not sure I believe in it. Not completely. It takes away the power of choice. I may not know exactly why I chose to pick up that ball, but I did choose it."

Shawn waited for a young mother and her two small children to pass by, then turned right into another side aisle.

The section was nearly empty of customers, to Shawn's relief, the only other person a teenaged girl in a store smock, crouched down over a pile of small boxes. She ran a hand-held blade along the containers to open them and slowly began to unwrap and place the new inventory onto the shelf in front of her. "What kind of message would you like on your card?" Shawn asked. He scanned the wide display in front of him. *"Congratulations on your new bundle of joy?* How about *Lordy Lordy Look who's forty?"* He laughed. The section was packed tightly with brightly colored paper greetings, a few empty spaces visible only in the graduation section. The crouching employee must have recently restocked it.

"I know you'll choose a lovely one." Helena's voice was quietly serious again. "But, listen, before we—"

"I've got it," said Shawn, picking up a bright pink card with a detailed illustration of a bird fleeing a cage on the front. *"You'll be sorely missed,"* he laughed. "Now, *this*—"

"Who are you talking to?" Maryann's sudden voice was much louder than Helena's had been. Firm. Angry.

Shawn turned to face her. "What? I was… What are you doing here?" He felt his face redden, his hand clutching the card frozen in mid-air.

"I followed you," Maryann said, her eyes not wavering

from his face. "You left for the store over an hour ago. So, I drove up here myself. I saw your car in the lot and parked and came in to look for you."

"Why?" Shawn slowly lowered the card.

"It's been over an hour," Maryann said. "You only had five things to pick up. I wanted to see if you were really here."

"You wanted to see if I was really here?" repeated Shawn. "Are you kidding?" He motioned around the aisle with his empty hand. "Have you seen the store? It's a madhouse. It's a holiday weekend, for Christ's sakes."

"That's not the only reason," Maryann said. Her eyes left his face and traveled down his arm to the hand clutching the card. "Who were you talking to? Where is your phone?"

"It's in my pocket. And no one." Shawn looked away, toward his shopping cart. Everything he set out to buy was piled neatly inside it.

Maryann swallowed. "Are you leaving me?" she asked, her voice abruptly hushed.

Shawn frowned, the guilt painted everywhere on his expression. "What? No. Why would you ask that?" Even as he said it, he wished he could take the words back. He knew their hollow tone damned him more than their empty meaning.

Maryann's countenance twisted. "Because if you do, you'll

be sorry," she spat, the softness having evaporated just as quickly as it had come.

Shawn placed the empty hand on his hip. "What does that mean?"

"It means, say goodbye to your house. Say goodbye to half your income," Maryann hissed. "And say goodbye to your sons. I will make certain you never see Tommy and Jessie again."

"Are you crazy?" Shawn yelled, catching himself and forcing his ire down into his stomach. "You and I both know," he growled between gritted teeth, "that you don't even like them. You hate being a mom, and now you're threatening to be one full-time? Good luck with that, Mae."

"I will do it," Maryann stage-whispered back, pointing her finger in her husband's face. "Just to make you miserable. I know you have someone else. I've *heard* you, Shawn. You think I'm an idiot?"

Shawn shook his head, but Maryann grabbed his wrist and pulled the hand clutching the greeting card closer. "Who is this for? And please: don't bother to lie about it."

Shawn tried to pull his hand back, but his wife's grip was firm. "Mae, let go," he pleaded, trying to keep his voice even. He grabbed her arm with his free hand and tried to wrestle himself free.

Maryann slapped her husband's shoulder over and over with her other hand in frustration, then finally unhinged her fingers and stepped sideways a pace. "You," she wagged her finger in his face again. "You will be sorry, Shawn. I am done. Do you hear me?" Her voice rose steadily in volume until Shawn was certain people in neighboring aisles could hear. "Done!" she continued, her pitch resembling nothing less than a wailing scream. "And I am taking the boys. You just try and stop me. You just—"

It took a moment for Shawn to process what was happening. One minute, his wife was yelling at him, her face twisted in a mixture of emotional hurt and aggressive anger; the next, her face had blanched and her frown and dejection were wiped clean, a pale canvas drained to emptiness like the top of an hourglass. Very slowly, her mouth clenched again, but this time, it was into a mangled o-shape, her eyes widening in surprise and disbelief, a hitched cry of pain leaking from her throat.

Shawn blinked, trying to clear his vision. The salesclerk was no longer crouched on the floor, unloading boxes. Somehow, at some point in their argument, she had risen and walked up behind them. Shawn watched in disbelief as the brown-haired girl drove her box-cutter into Maryann's stomach again and again, the blade making sickening wet shushing sounds under the faint hum of the store's fluorescent lighting with each entry and exit. The lower half of his wife's light blue t-shirt was quickly turning wet and black, drizzles of bright red blood splattering on the white speckled floor tiles and nearby metal shelving.

"No!" Shawn yelled. "No! No no no NO!" He pushed the clerk as hard as he could, knocking her to the ground, the girl's thick, black-framed glasses tumbling from her face, landing in a quiet clatter on the ground. Her face held an expression of astonishment as she brought both of her hands to her eyes to feel for the absent spectacles. The hand holding the weapon was painted completely with Maryann's blood, and a splotch of it smeared onto the girl's cheek as her wrist brushed against it. When she began to sit up, Shawn pounced on her and pushed her back onto the floor. As he did so, the box cutter tipped backwards and the girl accidentally stabbed her own face with the blade, the sharp edge implanting itself just above her right eyebrow. She jerked forward from the pain, and Shawn grabbed the wrist holding the cutter on instinct to protect himself, but he succeeded instead in pulling the blade further along the girl's skin, tearing open the delicate flesh all the way down to the rim of her eye socket.

It was a security guard who pulled Shawn to his feet and held him against the adjacent shelf while the paramedics and police arrived. He did not struggle, but he refused to take his eyes from the girl in the store smock as she lay silently dazed and bleeding against the same shelf, just a few feet away, a heavy cloth pressed firmly against her forehead by a store manager. "Shawn? Shawn?" Maryann repeatedly called to him as the emergency technicians lifted her efficiently onto a stretcher and wheeled his wife down the aisle and out of sight. He never moved his eyes to look at her, even as his wife's voice trailed away just as the sirens on the ambulance would, carrying her and her attacker to the hospital.

Despite his unbroken stare, it wasn't until the second set of paramedics lifted the girl onto her own stretcher that he saw it: the store name tag pinned neatly to her uniform. The brown-haired teenager's name was clearly spelled in black block letters.

Helena.

MARYANN SMILED DRUNKENLY from her hospital bed, her face appearing frail and small surrounded by the stark white pillow and linens. Shawn clutched her hand in his and smiled back. They had exchanged no words since the incident in the store that morning, and it seemed pointless to do so now when she was so close to nodding off, still dopey from remnants of the pain killer they'd administered.

A doctor, a young man obviously fresh out of medical school, wandered distractedly into the room, tapping a tablet balanced on a clipboard. "How are we doing?" he said brightly, though he did not look up.

Maryann blinked, then let her eyes droop closed. Shawn answered. "Okay, I think. She's really tired."

The doctor still did not make eye contact. "That's to be expected. The good news is, there doesn't seem to be any permanent damage. She's a lucky lady. A few inches higher and they could have punctured her stomach, ruptured the spleen." He made a note with a small stylus pen and tapped the screen with his index finger. "We anticipate less scarring than from her C-sections, too: she'll be happy to know." He looked up from his tablet and toward the large window next to Shawn. "It's strange to see the progress that's made every day." He nodded his head toward the view. Outside, a crane and two bulldozers were busy moving pieces of brick and land around the construction area, a new extension of the hospital building. Men in yellow vests and hardhats mingled about the machinery, some pointing or waving their arms in gesticulation. "Soon, the view will be completely different," he added.

Shawn looked at his unconscious wife. Her face was slack, void of any trace of the rage and vitriol that had erupted only a few hours earlier. He turned back to answer the young intern, but the doctor was already slipping back out into the hallway. Shawn sat back in the chair and glanced out of the window. The hook block on the crane swung back and forth through the air like a pendulum.

"Shawn?"

Helena's voice was so faint, Shawn questioned if he had imagined it. He squeezed his eyes tight, unsure of what to say.

"I don't know if you can hear me, or if you even want to, but I want to explain," she said.

"Okay," Shawn said. He tried to keep his eyes shut, but when he did, the image of Helena, young Helena, sitting in her bloodied store smock on the floor, her one uncovered eye fixed forward in shock, flashed across his vision.

"I don't know what made me do it," she said. "I've had nearly thirty years to think about it—and believe me, it has never escaped my mind, not for one single day—and I still don't know. I remember seeing the two of you argue, hearing the screaming, seeing her point her finger at you, and then… then it was happening. I just did it. Like the day I picked up the ball in the middle of—"

"I think this is a bit more serious than a child's soccer game," Shawn snapped. He looked at Maryann again. Her mouth was slightly open, her lips parted in a slight pout. Behind her closed lids, her eyes swam back and forth. Dreaming.

"Yes," Helena said. "It is. Much more serious. But…I can't explain it. The feeling was the same. The moment of relief at the silence that followed immediately after." She paused. "I—"

"You knew," Shawn said. "That's why I couldn't come to visit you. You knew you wouldn't be there… not yet."

"Right about now, I am on a transport bus to the prison. Seventeen-year old me, that is. They made certain to hasten my stitches, had an intern with no formal suture training sew me up, so that I could be booked and in a cell before the holiday." Shawn heard her sigh softly. "Forty-four-year-old me… she's still here, in the same cell block I've been in for decades."

"But how—"

"I don't know. How were we able to talk at all?" Both of them were silent for a moment, then Shawn heard her utter a tiny, sad, tinkling laugh. "I'd say I'll see you in thirty years, but, well, with the body replacing itself every seven…"

"We won't be the same," Shawn finished. He swallowed hard and looked at his wife, down at her hand, their gold wedding band encircling her finger.

"I'm so sorry. Please forgive me," Helena said.

Shawn turned toward the window and watched the crane lower its arm toward the ground. He felt inside his jacket pocket and pulled out the greeting card he'd numbly shoved inside before following his wife to the hospital. He ran his finger along the small spot of blood that had dried next to the illustration of the bird cage. *You'll be sorely missed.*

"Helena?" he whispered softly. But she was gone.

SHAWN PUSHED his empty glass forward and nodded at the bartender.

The woman with the bobbed hair smiled coyly. "You've been pulling my leg. You're a writer, aren't you?" When he said nothing in return, she touched his arm again. "I loved your story. Did the scientist ever find Helena, meet her in person, when she got older?"

The bartender placed a small piece of paper on the bar. "No," Shawn said, feeling in his jacket pocket for his billfold. "Even now, it will be another fifteen or so years before Helena becomes the woman he knew back then." He tossed a handful of crisp bills on top of the paper and returned the wallet to its hiding place beside his heart. "And by then, I suspect he will be a very different person than the man she knew. It's funny: out of all of the emotions that fade over time, somehow, regret never does. Maybe because it's the one feeling we can never repurpose." He shrugged.

"Did he mail the greeting card?" the woman asked.

Shawn looked down at his hands resting on the top of the bar. He smiled to himself but did not answer.

The woman squinted at him. "Do you wear lenses now?"

At this, Shawn chuckled. "I do. Soon after the series of Covid strains dissipated, I had to start wearing cheaters and increasing the strength nearly monthly. It finally got to the point where I was wearing glasses all the time, except to sleep, so I broke down and got fitted." He looked at his reflection in the mirror behind the stacks of cordials and liquors at the back of the bar. His hair was completely white. Even his eyebrows had only traces of dark in them, distant echoes of youth long gone.

The woman fixed her expression into a sad pout. "Too bad that CH-55 never panned out and you had to break down and get those contacts after all."

Shawn pushed himself from the stool and nodded a valediction. "Not too bad," he said. "If nothing else, I can finally see."

REBECCA ROWLAND

Characterized by *Rue Morgue Magazine* as "the fast-rising dark fiction talent who deftly wed[s] hardcore horror and true, affecting pathos," Rebecca Rowland is a Bram Stoker Award-nominated editor (*American Cannibal*) and a Shirley Jackson Award-nominated author (*White Trash & Recycled Nightmares*). In 2023, *Optic Nerve* snagged a Readers' Choice 666 Award from Godless Horror.

Despite her love of the ocean and distaste for cold weather, Rebecca makes her home in a landlocked and often icy corner of New England (USA). She is represented by Becky LeJeune of Bond Literary Agency. For more information, follow her on Instagram at Rebecca_Rowland_books or visit RowlandBooks.com.